WHEEZY'S WINGS

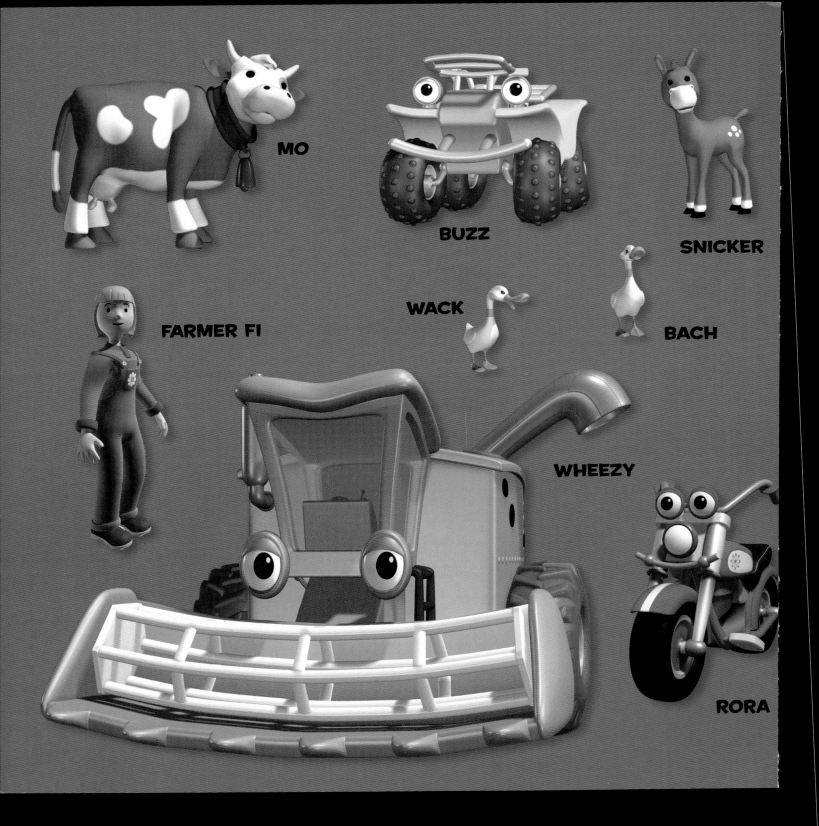

MO

BUZZ

SNICKER

FARMER FI

WACK

BACH

WHEEZY

RORA

DUSTY

THE HENS

PURDEY

REV

RIFF

THE SHEEP

MATT

WINNIE

TOM

First published in Great Britain by
HarperCollins Children's Books in 2005

1 3 5 7 9 10 8 6 4 2

ISBN: 0-00-719934-1

Text adapted from the original script by Andrew Brenner

48 Margaret Street London W1W 8SE

www.contendergroup.com

Tractor Tom © Contender Ltd 2002

A CIP catalogue record for this title is available from the British Library.

Printed and bound in China

WHEEZY'S WINGS

HarperCollins *Children's Books*

"Bark, bark, bark!"
Farmer Fi, Tractor Tom and Riff were trying to move the sheep across the stream into a new field. But the sheep didn't want to get wet. They wouldn't move.

"Can I help, Fi?" asked Dusty. "I have an idea."

Dusty said she would fly the sheep over the stream. The sheep liked this idea. They quickly lined up for a ride in Dusty.

"I wish I could fly!" sighed Rora. Rora, Tom and Buzz were watching Dusty fly the sheep over the stream.

"It's easy," said Dusty, coming in to land. "You just go really fast until you take off."

Tom, Rora and Buzz all went really fast. But they couldn't get off the ground.

"*Zoom, zoom!*"

"Why are you all rushing up and down?" asked Rev.

"We're trying to fly!" said Buzz. "Would you like to try, Rev?"

Rev said he didn't need to try, he could already fly. Trucks could do anything! And he would show them.

"Could I have a little help, please?" Rev whispered to Tom.

"But I thought trucks could do anything!" laughed Tom.

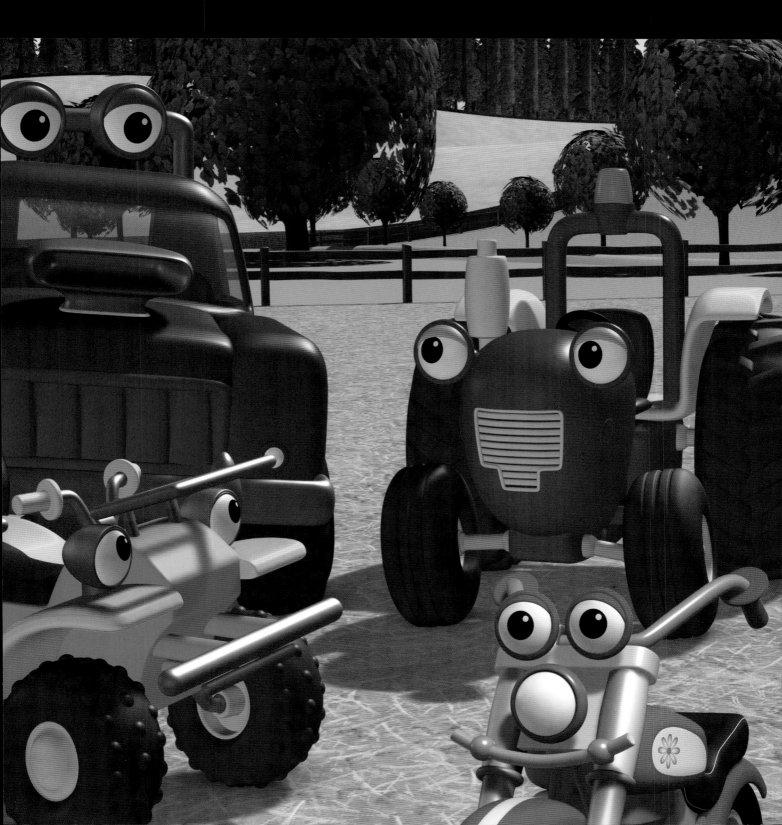

First Rev showed Buzz, Rora and Tom how to build a ramp. Next, Rev zoomed up the ramp and *flew* off the top!

"Yee-haw! I'm flying!" cried Rev.
"That's not flying. That's jumping!" said Rora. But Buzz didn't mind.

"Wheeeee!" he shouted, as he went flying off the ramp.
He even went further than Rev. Rev wasn't very happy.

Soon Rora and Tom were 'flying' too!
Everybody was having a great time. Everybody
except Wheezy.

"Come on, Wheezy. Why don't you have a
go?" asked Tom.
"I don't think I'd be very good at flying," said
Wheezy, sadly.
"You won't know unless you try," replied Tom.

"Ok, Tom. I'll try,"
Wheezy said.
But he didn't
sound very sure.

At the stream Dusty was still moving the sheep.
  "Next," she called.
  The naughty sheep were using a secret bridge
to run back across the stream. They wanted lots
of flights in Dusty.

  Flying with Dusty looked so much fun even Mo
the cow wanted a turn.
  "Mo-oooooo!"
But poor Mo got stuck in Dusty's cockpit!
  "That's it," sighed Dusty. "No more rides."

Wheezy took a big breath and started to roll up the ramp. He wasn't going very fast. He got to the top then.... CRASH!

Wheezy fell off the end of the ramp.

"I told you I was no good, Tom," he said.
"Don't worry, Wheezy. If you want to fly then we'll help you," encouraged Tom. Rora, Buzz and Rev cheered, "yeah!"

Buzz had an idea, "I know, Wheezy. You need wings like Dusty."

The friends got some old planks and tied them onto Wheezy. Now Wheezy had wings!

"Go really fast down Beckton Hill and then over the bridge. You will definitely take off," Rev told Wheezy.

So Wheezy went really fast down Beckton Hill and over the bridge. But he didn't take off.

Buzz, Rev, Rora and Tom huddled around
Wheezy.
   "Couldn't you pull Wheezy into the sky, Tom?"
asked Buzz.

   "Don't be silly
Buzz. I'm the
strongest vehicle
on the farm and
I couldn't do that!"
said Rev, proudly.

   This gave Tom an idea. Rev couldn't *pull*
Wheezy into the sky, but he could *carry* him.
   "That's true, Buzz," said Tom. "Rev couldn't
pull Wheezy."

"Of course I could pull Wheezy, Tom. Trucks can do anything!" Rev boasted. He didn't want anyone to think he couldn't do something.
"Could you *carry* Wheezy?" asked Tom.
"Of course!" replied Rev.

So Tom and his friends built another ramp and Wheezy rolled onto Rev's back.
"I'm not sure about this, Tom," said Wheezy.
"Don't worry, Wheezy," said Tom. "I'll pull Rev."

"Wheee! I'm flying!" called Wheezy.

Tom, Rev and Wheezy were racing across the fields.

"Looks like Rev is the one giving rides now!" laughed Dusty.

The sheep thought Rev's rides looked like lots of fun too. They ran across the bridge.

"Look, Dusty," said Fi. "The sheep are on the right side of the stream!"

"Wow, Rev. Thanks!" gasped Wheezy.
"That was brilliant! I really did fly."
  "Well done, Rev. You really are very strong,"
Tom smiled.

  "Oooh. My aching axles!" groaned Rev.
  "Gah!" The sheep had jumped on Rev's back.
  "The sheep want to fly with Rev too!"
laughed Tom.

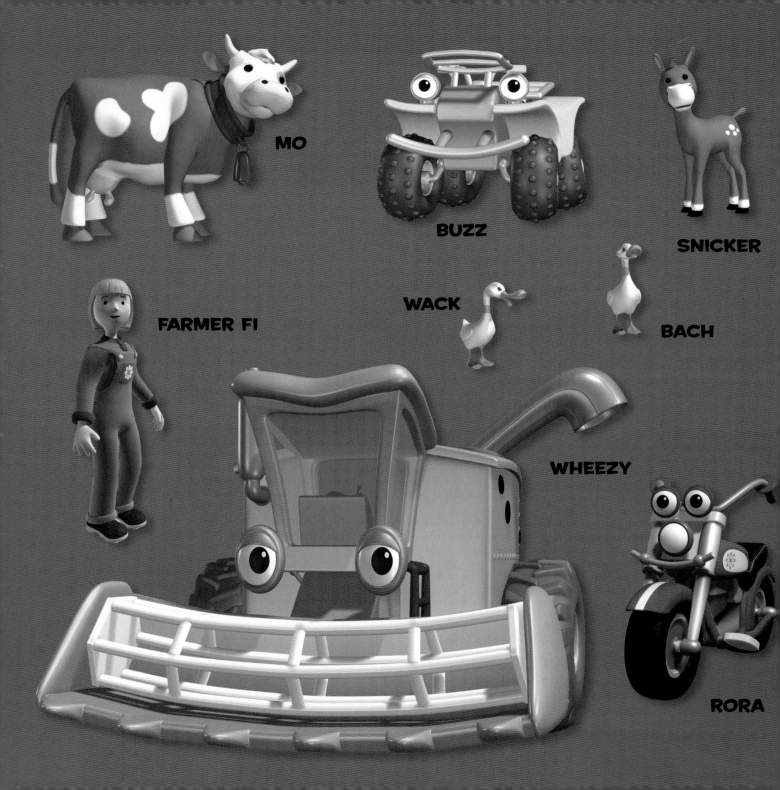

MO

BUZZ

SNICKER

FARMER FI

WACK

BACH

WHEEZY

RORA

DUSTY

THE HENS

PURDEY

REV

RIFF

THE SHEEP

TOM

WINNIE

MATT

YOU CAN COLLECT THEM ALL!

1-84357-066-1 £3.99 — TRACTOR TOM'S ACTIVITY BOOK

1-84357-064-5 £3.99 — TRACTOR TOM AND THE MOBILE PHONE

1-84357-065-3 £3.99 — TRACTOR TOM'S "WHERE'S IT GONE?" STICKER BOOK

1-84357-087-4 £3.99 — TRACTOR TOM'S SPORTS DAY

0-00-718904-4 £5.99 — MY TRACTOR TOM PLAYBOOK
FIND AND FIT THE SHAPES TO HELP TRACTOR TOM ON THE FARM!

0-00-718900-1 £3.99 — TREASURE TRAIL

0-00-718901-X £3.99 — A SURPRISE FOR FI

0-00-718902-8 £3.99 — BAA BAA TOM SHEEP

0-00-718903-6 £3.99 — A JOB FOR BUZZ

WWW.TRACTORTOM.COM

TRACTOR TOM

WHAT WOULD WE DO WITHOUT HIM?